190

D1002294

HOP-HIGH

HOP-HIGH,
The Goat

written and illustrated by

Laura Bannon

the NEW *Bobbs-Merrill* COMPANY, INC.
AN ASSOCIATE OF **HOWARD W. SAMS & CO., INC.**
Publishers • INDIANAPOLIS • NEW YORK

Copyright © 1960 by the Bobbs-Merrill Company, Inc.
Printed in the United States of America

First Edition

Library of Congress Catalog Card Number: 60-6939

A Navaho
Story of a
Mischievous Goat

We are bouncing along in our wagon
dressed in our best clothes. Mother is
wearing her new blouse trimmed with
rows of money pieces. She holds the
umbrella and lets me hold our baby,
Little-Last-One. Father is driving.

7

We sing a good luck song for a safe journey to the trading post. I have a true voice. That is why I am called Singing Girl.

I stop singing to cry out, "Here comes Aunt Many-Goats."

My aunt is on a horse and is driving a flock of sheep. We notice that a goat in her flock is butting her sheep dog. My aunt hits at the goat with her reins to make him stop.

"That goat!" she says when she is close by. "Even his own mother could not be bothered with that one. I had to raise him myself, and he is spoiled."

I see that the goat is young and full of fun. He springs straight up and down. He butts everything he comes to.

I climb down the wagon wheel to pet him. I scratch him behind the ear, and he nibbles my cheek.

"He is beautiful," I say. "I like him. And see, he likes me."

"Then you may have him," my aunt says.

I thank her. I am not too much surprised, because it is this aunt who gave me the sheep that leads my mother's flock, and she gave me my peach tree that grows

down in the canyon. I am not too much surprised, but I am plenty pleased to own this goat. I think maybe my father is not so pleased. As we ride on to the trading post, he says, "A spoiled goat can give much trouble."

I stay in the back of the wagon to play with the goat. He keeps climbing on the roll of sheepskins just for the fun of jumping off. He jumps so high I begin to call him Hop-High.

He knows I am laughing at him, even when I hold the laugh inside until it shakes me.

At the trading post, we tie the horses alongside Mr. Hurry-Up's garden fence. He is the white man who runs the store.

While Mother is climbing down the wagon wheel, she takes a look over the fence at Mr. Hurry-Up's garden. "He has beautiful first-flowers-of-spring," she tells us.

Father hands the sheepskins and the bags of wool down to Mother. We have many of them to sell. This is a good thing, because today we need to buy a lot of food to take with us down into the canyon for the summer.

I leave Hop-High in the wagon and help carry our goods into the store.

Many of our people, the Navahos, are standing together in the middle of the storeroom. Mr. Hurry-Up is showing them a big basket on wheels.

He explains that the basket
is a holding place for a baby.
He can talk nice.

11

Mother says, "This basket would keep our little one away from the bite of the big red ant."

I bounce the basket on its springs and say, "I could keep our baby happy in this."

Then Mr. Talks-Much, who is watching, speaks up. "Let's see how a Navaho baby likes this white man's baby basket," he says.

Mother unlaces the strings of the babyboard and lays Little-Last-One in the soft holding place. He squints his eyes shut and opens his mouth wide. *"A-wah! A-wah! A-wah!"* he howls.

Everyone laughs, and Mr. Talks-Much says, "He knows what is best for a Navaho baby."

Our baby is too new to want anything but his babyboard, we think.

Now Mr. Hurry-Up explains all about a stove he has to sell. It is a great bargain, he tells Father.

Father says, "Tomorrow we move down into Rock Canyon. To take this stove with us would be much trouble."

"Leave it in the hogan," Mr. Hurry-Up says. "You will be glad to have it when you come back in the fall. Today I am almost giving it to you, because I can't have it in my way all summer."

I do not wait to see what is decided about the stove. I run out to see how about Hop-High.

I climb into the wagon and what don't I see? I don't see Hop-High. He is nowhere in the wagon. He is gone.

But I have an ache inside me. This goat was mine for only a little while, but now I cannot be happy without him. He was so filled with fun.

I stand high up on the wagon seat and call to him. I look everywhere about, even over the fence into Mr. Hurry-Up's garden.

Do I see a flip of a tail inside the fence? Yes, I do. It is Hop-High. He has jumped from the wagon, over the fence and into the flowers.

Holah! Hop-High is eating a whole row of beautiful flowers. I run fast, you can bet. I grab that rascal and hustle him out through the gate. Does he act sorry? No. He bounces and butts at me and wants to play.

14

Mother and Father are coming out of the store with boxes of groceries. Mother is saying, "It has a fine bounce and will be useful later on."

And I say, "Oh, yes. He is a smart one. He will grow into a fine big goat."

Mother laughs and says, "Since when will a basket on wheels grow into a fine big goat?"

Now I understand that they are talking about the bouncing basket and not about Hop-High. They are trying to decide whether to buy the stove or the basket.

When I boost Hop-High into the wagon, I tie him up. But I give him plenty of rope to move around. I explain, "For now, he is a little bad about running away. But that is only because he is too young to want to stay still."

Mother says, "Where did you find the goat?"

"Beside Mr. Hurry-Up's fence," I say. I do not lie. This is a true telling.

We sit in the wagon shade and eat crackers and drink pop.

Father says, "We won't have another chance to buy a stove for so little money."

Mother says, "It not only has a holding place for the

15

fire and a going away place for the smoke, but it has a holding place for food, too. The tight door would keep out ants and bugs. I think it is a good thing to buy."

It is settled. Mr. Hurry-Up helps load the stove into the wagon. Then he says good-by to us and goes back to the store.

Mother is the last to get into the wagon. She climbs up the wheel and stops to have a last look at Mr. Hurry-Up's nice garden.

She is very still.

Is she missing the flowers?

I hold my breath.

"On which side of the fence did you find your goat?" she asks.

"On the inside," I say, and my voice comes out small.

"It is like stealing to go away and do nothing about this," she says.

She climbs down and goes into the store. When she comes back, some of the money pieces are gone from her beautiful new blouse.

I am crying on the inside as I ride along, sitting between Mother and Father.

Then, without looking around, I can tell what Hop-High is doing. I can tell by the rattle and bangs that the rascal is climbing on top of the iron stove and jumping off. I gave him too much rope, I think. But soon Father does look around. *"Holah!"* he cries out, "Look what that mud-head goat is up to now!"

I look and what do I see? Hop-High is butting a
hole in a sack of flour. The flour leaks out in a white
river. I am quick to climb back to him.

Mother says to me, "Take the umbrella and put the
sack in it. Save what flour you can."

This I do. While I am
stooped over, Hop-High
gives me a butt from be-
hind and tips me headfirst
into the flour. I come out
with a face as white as snow.

Now even Father has to
laugh. But he says, "Tie
that mudhead on a short
rope."

This I do, and Hop-High
becomes a good goat. He
sleeps most of the way
home.

Near the end of the trail, we see smoke rising out of the smoke hole of my mother's hogan. We sing the hogan song to warn Grandfather of our coming. We know he will put the coffee over the fire for us.

When we drive up, I let down the endgate of the wagon and pull Hop-High out. I take him into the hogan to show him to Grandfather.

He smiles and says, "I can see that this is a fine, smart goat." Grandfather can see good in everything.

Mother has taken the coffeepot off the fire that burns in the middle of the floor. The pot now stands to one side so she can fry bread.

Father is about to pour coffee into his tin cup. Just then, before anyone can stop him, Hop-High wheels and butts over the coffeepot. All the coffee spills across the earth floor.

"This mudhead goat is too much," Father shouts. "I think he would be better off in the stew kettle."

Mother slowly measures sugar and coffee in her hand and pours it into the coffee pot. "My child," she says, "you must keep the goat out of this hogan."

I lead Hop-High to the pen behind the hogan and put him with my mother's sheep.

When I come back, I see Grandfather standing by the wagon, looking at the stove. "So now we hide our cheerful fire inside this white man's hardware," he says.

While we eat supper we make plans for our trip down into Rock Canyon.

Every year the grass up on our mesa turns brown. The springs dry up. So we take our sheep and go for the summer down into this canyon we love.

There, the sands blow over the big snows of winter and hold them. Then in the moon-of-many-flowers, the snows melt and help the green things to grow.

It is decided that in the morning, after breakfast, Grandfather and I will go ahead of the others and follow the sheep. Father and Mother will pack our goods into the wagon and catch up with us in time to help drive the sheep down the steep pass into the canyon.

We all lie on our sheepskins and go to sleep. But suddenly my eyes and ears are very much open.

I hear a big racket outside the hogan. What is that
noise? It sounds as if something is knocking down
the brush that fences in the sheep.

And who could be doing that? *Holah!* Who knows?
Maybe a coyote or a wolf. But it could be that full of
mischief Hop-High, I think.

I am much afraid to go out in that dark. But what
if Hop-High should let out my mother's sheep to be

lost in the night? For that he would
end up in the stew kettle, I know.

When I creep outdoors, Hop-High
comes bouncing to me. I know him
by his white spots that show up in
the dark. Behind him, the sheep step
through the big hole he has butted
in the side of the pen.

"You are a bad one who thinks only good of yourself," I tell Hop-High. I shove him back through the hole. The sheep follow in a long line. I am making the fence strong again. When I look up, there is Father with his blanket wrapped around him.

He says nothing. He just pounds the stakes of the fence deeper into the ground.

I hurry into the hogan and try to fill myself with sleep before he comes back. I do not want to talk with him about Hop-High.

But behind my closed eyes I am awake. I am trying to think of ways to keep Hop-High out of the stew kettle until he gets old enough to act wiser.

The next thing I know, Mother is saying, "Come, everyone. The day is calling."

I open my eyes. It is the time-of-first-light. Grandfather rolls out of his blanket and sings:

"White light of dawning, she stirs, she stirs.
In the land of dawning, she stirs."

Little-Last-One sleeps on. It makes no difference to him that the dawning, she stirs.

Mother tells Father, "We have to move the stove into the hogan before we leave. If we bring it in now, I can cook our breakfast on it."

She cannot wait until fall to try out that new stove, I think.

I run to see how about Hop-High. He bounces and butts at me. He holds still only when I scratch him behind the ear.

Every morning it is my job to graze the sheep near by

27

while Mother is getting breakfast. I find the rattler hanging by the sheep gate. I made this rattler by putting pebbles into a tin can. Now I twirl it on a string to start the sheep.

They give me no trouble. They slowly follow my lead sheep and eat as they walk through the patches of rabbit brush.

But that Hop-High! He is everywhere. It takes all my time to keep him with the flock. I am glad when Grandfather comes out to help me.

After awhile, we hear Father calling, *"A-ya-an-na!"* We know he is out finding his horses that have been left free for the night to graze.

The new stove is set up, we think. Yes, there is the smoke tube poking out the top of the hogan. We watch for the smoke to come through it.

"Hulah!" Grandfather says. "Now that we have a white man's stove, the smoke from our fire comes out the hogan door."

This is true. Smoke rolls out in a black cloud. Has that stove set our hogan on fire? We see Father run toward it.

I start the flock back to the pen with my rattler.

Grandfather hustles Hop-High
along by holding one of his ears.
This is no time to have trouble
with that goat.

Mother comes out the door carrying Little-Last-One. "This stove is no good," she says between coughs. "It is of no use. It only trims the hogan like money pieces on a blouse."

Father is in the hogan seeing what is wrong. When he comes out, his eyes are crying from the smoke. But he is laughing.

"You have built the fire in the holding place for food," he tells Mother. "Where is the fire shovel? When I move the fire to the right place, the smoke will find the going-away-place."

He does this, and soon we see puffs of smoke from the top of the hogan. We all laugh at Mother, and she laughs, too, and feels silly.

It turns out that this is a good stove after all. Mother makes coffee on it and fries bread at the same time. And for a treat we open a can of store-bought peaches.

But Grandfather says, "In the moon-of-snows the sun goes to sleep early. We will sit in the dark while the light of our fire is shut inside this iron box."

We decide not to worry about that now. Mother begins to pack the balls of yarn for her weaving into a big basket.

I put on all the clothes I have.
My best skirt and blouse I wear
on the outside. And I wear my
earrings and beads and bracelets.

Before sundown time, we will see old friends who also come to the canyon for the summer.

Grandfather puts on his shoes with a hole cut out for his bunion. And soon we are following the flock.

At first all is beautiful. We walk slowly behind the sheep, and they graze as they walk. Hop-High is content to walk with the others and find grass for his empty stomach.

Grandfather and I are singing. Grandfather is called Old-Singer because he knows as many songs as there are cones on the little pine tree. He even makes up new songs.

I am a rich girl because I not only own a peach tree and a lead sheep and a fine goat—I also own a good-luck song. Grandfather made it and gave it to me.

Now I sing my song:

> "The earth is my mother,
> And I am her child.
> May all be beautiful.
> May I be a sharing child,
> And all will be beautiful."

Now Hop-High begins to give us trouble. He will not keep his place in the flock.

All the sheep have their places. Some stay up close to my lead sheep. After them come the middlers, and then the tailers come last.

But that Hop-High! He must be at the very front. Some of the sheep think they should follow him. *Hulah!* Who knows where that rascal will lead them? I run from side to side using the rattler. But I cannot keep the flock together.

We see our horses and wagon coming behind us in a cloud of dust. When Father overtakes us, he shouts, "Tie that goat behind the wagon!"

This I do.

Grandfather's bunion is bothering him by now. He climbs into the wagon and holds Little-Last-One. Mother helps me drive the flock down the long steep path into the canyon.

Father comes up close behind us. He walks and leads the horses.

Hop-High is bleating. Poor Hop-High! What goat likes to be yanked along by a rope around the neck?

I am having trouble with the lead sheep. She will not go down steep places. I go ahead and give her a push. When she goes, the other sheep follow.

Down, down we go.
We leave the wide sky
behind us. Now it is a
long blue ribbon high
over our heads.

34

At last we are down on the clean flat floor of Rock Canyon.

We are filled with happiness. We stop to eat in the cool shade of a cottonwood tree.

Then I see the awful thing that has happened. Hop-High is gone. Rope and all, he is gone. My heart sits inside me like a stone. I want to go back to find him.

"This is useless," Father tells me. "Do you think that goat will lie on a rock and wait for you? Maybe he is on his way back to Aunt Many-Goat's flock."

Once again, I find I cannot be happy without Hop-High. He was so full of bounce and play. I cry inside while I follow the sheep with Mother. I am thinking of that rope I tied around Hop-High's neck. He could hang himself with it, I worry.

Then I see an old friend come racing on his pony. His name is Bego-eskish. In Navaho, this means Gap-Between-The-Teeth. But in the winter school he is called John, and so that is what I call him.

Now I stroke his pony, Swift-Foot, while I tell John the sad story about Hop-High.

John is sad with me. "It would be fun for us to have a smart goat to play with," he says. "Sheep are dumb,

but a goat knows which way he is going."

Then John says, "See you tomorrow,"
and gallops away.

When we come to a turn in the canyon
wall, we see the place where we build
our shelter every summer. Father is already there with our load of goods. I
climb into the wagon to help unload.

Holah! I see a sight that makes my heart sing. At the back of the wagon is Mother's big basket of yarn. Asleep in this soft bed is Hop-High. He is still tied by the rope. I can see what has happened. He has jumped off a rock into the wagon. The rope got pulled in with him. Smart little Hop-High!

I put my arms around him, and he nibbles my cheek. I know he likes me.

Then I remember to hustle him out of the basket before Mother sees where he has been sleeping.

Mother and Father are surprised to see Hop-High jump out of the wagon. Even Father has to say that this is a wise goat.

Father mends last summer's sheep pen. Grandfather sings while he plugs the holes in the old storehouse with sticks and mud. Mother and I build a fire of twigs and cook a hot supper. Before it is ready, hunger sits inside us all.

Tonight we wrap ourselves in our blankets and sleep under the stars. From deep in the canyon, they look big, like sunflowers in the velvet sky.

By the cold-light-before-dawn, we are all awake. There is much to do. A new shelter must be built.

But my job is to graze the sheep. This is easy in the canyon. In most parts, the way between the canyon wall is narrow, and the sheep cannot scatter far. My heart sings as I follow them along the cool shadows of the cliffs.

I guide them to the place where my peach tree grows. This patch of land is now farmed by a Navaho who is new in the valley. But the peach tree still belongs to me.

There it is—a cloud of pink blossoms. In my heart I give it a song as Grandfather would:

> "You hold your blossoms high,
> away from me.
> But when the peaches are ripe,
> your branches will bend down to me,
> finished in beauty."

I keep the words inside me because I see John racing down the canyon on Swift-Foot. And I must show my goat to him at once.

Hop-High is gobbling fresh green grass, but when John pushes him between the horns he begins to play rough. John likes this. They battle together until they are both tired out.

Then John and I dig a deep hole in the sand and watch it fill with clean water. We line the hole with stones. It makes a fine little well, and Hop-High takes a drink from it.

I love my summer in Rock Canyon. While the sheep graze, I have time to play with the other children who have shelters near by. Hop-High plays with all of us.

He can play tag and also a game of
pushing us off a rock. Even the biggest
boys who race along the canyon on their
ponies stop to battle in fun with my
goat. Everybody likes him—everybody but Father.

While Hop-High is at home, I keep
him shut in the storehouse most of the
time. But he watches for his chance to
dash into the shelter.

This morning he grabs a ball of Mother's yarn. By the time we get it away from him, it is unwound and strung all over the camp.

Mother asks, "How can I sell a rug made with dirty yarn?"

Father is full of anger. "Now the time has come to do something about this mudhead," he says.

I don't want to hear more. I hustle Hop-High away to graze with the sheep in the yellow rabbit brush.

43

When John comes agalloping, he
sits for awhile with me, and I tell
him my troubles. I ask, "How can
we keep Hop-High out of the
stew kettle?"

John says, "I have to be alone to
think. You can take a ride on
Swift-Foot."

This I like to do. I gallop the
pony along the canyon walls until
my hair comes untied and flies out
behind me.

When I'm back, John sits with his arm around Hop-High, and he says he has the answer. "Give Hop-High to me," he says.

I tell him, "Think up another answer. I don't like the first one." I race off again on Swift-Foot.

When I'm back, John has a different answer. "Goat meat is tough," he says. "Mutton is better to eat. Give the lead sheep to your Father for the stew kettle and let Hop-High be leader. Already the sheep like to follow him."

"I'm afraid my Father will say that Hop-High is too young and foolish to lead," I tell John.

"Say nothing to your Father now," John tells me. "Just keep Hop-High out of mischief. Every day, while he is growing older, we will teach him to lead the sheep."

We try to follow this plan. Sometimes we graze my lead sheep in a different spot. Then we watch to see how well the sheep are following Hop-High.

But in the canyon, the sheep do not have to walk for miles to find food and water the way they do up on the mesa. Most of the time it is hard to tell who is doing the leading.

The summer passes like the white-
tailed rabbit racing before the wind.
Mother has finished weaving a big
rug to sell to Mr. Hurry-Up. The corn
that Father planted now stands in
thick clumps.

Mother makes ones-bent-over-at-the-
tips out of the green corn. To do this,
she mashes the corn until it is milky.
Then she fills the clean inside husks
of the ear with this batter and bends
the tips to hold in the batter.
After the corn is baked in the earth
pit, it is brown all over and so good.

We have come to the time of year when almost every day we hear the voice of thunder in the faraway mountains. And now it comes roaring across the canyon and brings the quick rains. We have to stack goods in our storeroom to keep them dry.

Today while we are eating, water trickles through the shelter onto us. And then by the time we finish eating, the rain is suddenly over.

We put our spoons into the empty kettle and watch Grandfather try to make Little-Last-One laugh out loud.

The first one to get a Navaho baby to laugh out loud has the honor of giving him a present. Grandfather claps his hands and says, "I'll give you a soft pair of moccasins if you will laugh for me."

The little one is sober.

Father tries. He makes silly faces. "Laugh for me," he says.

I do not know what he promises, because just then I happen to look at the storehouse. There is Hop-High standing on top of it. He is covered with mud. He must have climbed up on something and butted a hole in the roof where the rain has made it soft, I think.

I have to get over there and tie him up. For an excuse I say, "I'll get my rattler. That will make Little-Last-One laugh out loud."

I jump up and start toward the storehouse. My eyes are on that rascal Hop-High. My feet stumble over the kettle. It rattles with the spoons—rattles loud and plenty. I go sprawling in front of the little sober one.

And what happens? He makes a beautiful laugh with his voice. This is a true telling. I am not even trying to do so, yet I get the first laugh.

Now everybody but me laughs. I do well not to cry, because I have hurt my knee on the kettle.

"You have the honor of giving the first-laugh gift," Mother tells me.

Hop-High takes all this to be a game, I think. He comes bouncing down to me, kicking up his heels.

He spatters mud all over Mother's beautiful rug. This is a bad, bad thing.

Mother yells, *"Su! Su!,"* and chases him away. She scowls and begins to pick specks of mud off the rug.

Now Mudhead is not a bad enough name for Hop-High. Father thinks up new ones. And he says he will not put up with this loco goat any longer.

"No fence or wall will hold this loco mudhead for long," he says. "You will keep him around until he loses your mother's sheep. The only safe place for him is in the stew kettle."

I say, "Put the lead sheep in the stew kettle and let Hop-High lead the sheep. Goat meat is tough."

"And what is wrong with tough meat?" roars Father. "Tough meat keeps hunger away longer. It is not the lead sheep who is meant for the kettle."

I take Hop-High out behind a rock where no one can see us. I am crying inside, but not because my knee hurts.

After a long time, when it is dark and chilly, Mother finds me there. She tells me, "Animals should be used as they serve best."

"But Hop-High could serve better as a leader than my lead sheep," I say. "He is smarter."

"Smartness is not all that counts," Mother tells me. "Smartness can lead down the wrong trail as well as the right one. You might sell your goat to Mr. Hurry-Up," she says. "You could buy yourself a pretty new blouse with the money."

"I would rather have Hop-High," I say.

"You would have enough money left to buy the first-laugh gift," Mother tells me. "Giving is good medicine for pushing unhappiness out of the heart."

"But I wasn't trying to make Little-Last-One laugh."

That night I have bad dreams.
When I wake at sunup-time, a
stone sits inside me. I know this
is because I am selfish. I am not
a sharing child on my mother-
earth as my song says I am.

I say to Mother, "I will sell
Hop-High to Mr. Hurry-Up."

When I take the sheep to graze, I turn them down a side canyon. There I will be alone. I do not want to talk to anyone, not even my friend, John.

I sit on a rock and watch Hop-High grazing with the flock.

The sun pushes his way up the sky and comes to the middle. But he has lost his fierce light. He goes behind a cloud.

Little whirlwinds of sand come spinning up the canyon. The sheep are not happy.

Maybe I should start them toward home, I think. I twirl my rattler to guide them back up the canyon. But the breezes have changed to a strong talking wind. And sheep do not like to have the wind blow into their wool from the back. The lead sheep runs in circles with the flock.

Now the above-world turns black and dumps its water into the canyon. Waterfalls tumble down the cliff. This will flood the floor of the canyon and drown my mother's sheep, I think.

Hop-High starts up the rocks to a higher place in the side of the canyon wall. Some of the sheep follow him. I run over and push the slow ones to keep them climbing.

At last the sheep are all safe from the flood, I think, and so I follow. But this is not true. I look down and

see the lead sheep on a low
ledge. With her is a half-
grown lamb. Now the
canyon floor is a fast river.
Branches tumble along in
the foam. I cannot get over
to the sheep on the ledge.

I sit with my arms around Hop-High.
But I sing to all the sheep to keep them
quiet and I cry a little.

Soon the rain stops. It is running
off and sinking into the sand. I see
that the lead sheep is still on the low
ledge. But she stands alone. The lamb
is gone. I have lost one of my mother's
sheep. My heart is like a stone.

My selfish thoughts have made all of
this trouble, I think.

Then someone calls. Father rides out
of the mist on his horse. "Father," I
call. "I have lost one of the sheep."

I am on the horse, sitting in front of Father. We are riding slowly behind the flock. The sheep make sharp holes in the smooth sand with their hoofs. I watch the holes fill with water.

As soon as I can make the words come, I explain:

"When the floods came, Hop-High led the other sheep to higher land. But

that stupid lead sheep would not follow, and the lamb stayed with her. I didn't see them in time. The water was too deep for me to get them. When the rain stopped the lamb was gone. I couldn't help it."

"All is beautiful," Father tells me. "All that we care for most came through the flood alive."

I see Hop-High out in front of the flock. All the sheep, even the leader, follow him. I think Father now cares for Hop-High, too.

We have come to the moon-of-leaves-turning-yellow.
We pick the little sweet peaches from my tree. Mother
cuts some of them in two and dries them in the sun, so
they will keep. We pack our corn in boxes to take to
our winter hogan.

I say good-by to my friends. To John I say, "See you
later in the winter school." In my heart I say good-by
to my peach tree and to this canyon I love—good-by
until next moon-of-many-flowers.

Our wagon is loaded high. The horses have a long
hard pull up the pass, out of the canyon.

But all the sheep follow
Hop-High up the rocks.
He leads them across the
mesa to our winter hogan.

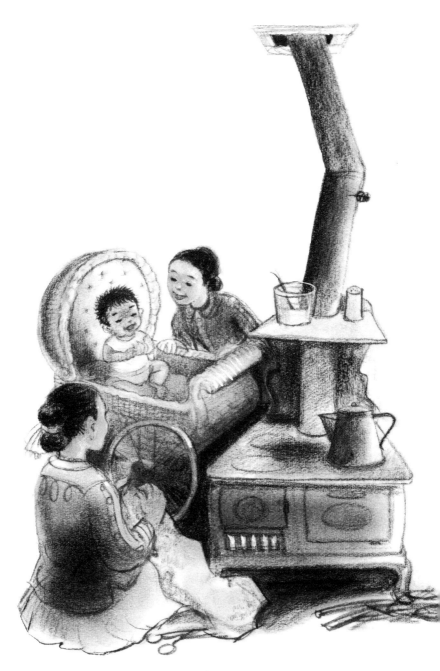

Now the thunder sleeps in the mountains. Frost stays all day in the hogan shadow. We sit inside, around our warm stove. And we have enough light because Father bought a white man's lantern.

I am watching Mother make my new purple velvet blouse. And I am getting Little-Last-One to laugh by bouncing him in his basket. Yes, we have the baby basket on wheels. I bought it for the first-laugh gift. And I had money enough left for the blouse cloth. I paid for them by selling the lead sheep to Mr. Hurry-Up.

How about Hop-High?

When he is with the sheep, he is
the smartest leader in all Navaho
land. But sometimes he is still a
clown. Tonight he butted over the
water barrel. But no one called him
names. We just laughed and ate
our supper without coffee.

Orchard School Library

Bannon, Laura   Copy 2

Hop-High, The Goat

Fj
Ban

                         Copy 2

OC 23'72